The Unexpected Love Story of Alfred Fiddleduckling

TIMOTHY BASIL ERING

WALKER BOOKS
AND SUBSIDIARIES
LONDON · BOSTON · SYDNEY · AUCKLAND

 aptain Alfred was sailing home.

On his little boat, there were new ducks for
his farm and, nestled safe inside his fiddle case,
a precious gift for his wife.

It was a beautiful duck egg that
was very close to hatching.

"A ducklin' born in *my* fiddle case must be named
Alfred Fiddleducklin'!" Captain Alfred said with a giggle.
"You're goin' to be a very special little ducklin',"
Captain Alfred told the egg.

But something unexpected was coming.

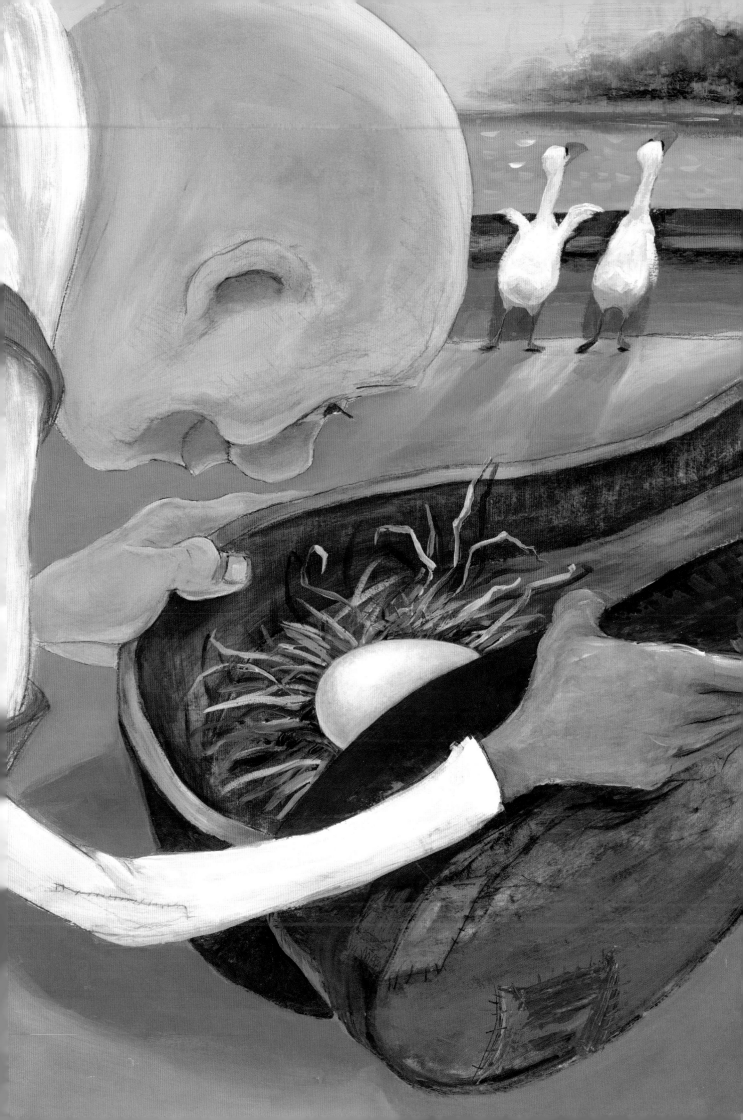

It was a storm.

A big one.

A sudden and mighty gale
whipped the seas into a raging fury.

After an endless hour of howling wind and tossing seas …

there was silence.

No waves. No wind.

A blanket of fog
covered everything.

Hidden in the whiteness as thick as pea soup
sat a little cottage overlooking the bay.

On the porch stood a gentle lady in a grey wool coat.

Tears of worry dropped from her cheeks, into the mist.

Yet far offshore, deep in the fog, alone and drifting,
the egg cracked.

No one was there to hug little Alfred
when he stumbled out of his shell.

But there *was* an object,
floating not too far away in the waves.

Alfred quacked.

The object did not
quack back.

Alfred swam up to it.

It did not reach out to him.

But Alfred embraced the object
with all of his heart.

And he caressed it so it would not feel
as lonely as he did.

Then something unexpected happened…

The object made the most beautiful
sound Alfred had ever heard.

Alfred loved the object!

And, by the sound of its beautiful music,
the object loved Alfred, too.

They drifted through the fog,
over wave after wave, playing together until…

Bump! Alfred felt something touch his feet.

They had landed at a very mysterious place.

Alfred held the object close.

"Don't be afraid," he said.

And in a few moments,
the soft, comforting sounds
began again.

The sounds drifted on through the foggy reeds
until they reached the very keen ears of a beast
that was lurking in the tall grasses.

The beast's heart pounded. How unexpected!
He wanted to follow those sounds.

He charged through the fog ...

and found them!

Drool dripped from the beast's jaw.
It leaned in even closer.

Alfred trembled with fear –

and his music became fast and wild!

The huge beast lifted its front paws high into the air
until it was standing tall on its hind legs.

And then, suddenly …

that big old beast started to dance!

Captain Alfred's lost dog had longed for the sounds of
his master's fiddle. He, too, had been very lonely.

Now, in just a twinkle of an eye,
the duckling and the dog were best buddies.

Being lost with a friend was much better
than being lost alone.

Sadly, though, lost was lost.
As the hours stretched by,
the friends grew cold.

Wet.
Helpless.

The tiny quivering music left in the object
was not enough to boost their spirits.

But that tiny sound *was* enough
to excite the ears of …

the gentle lady wearing the grey wool coat
who was praying for her husband, her dog,
and the new ducks for their farm
to return home safely.

She ran through the fog,
straight towards the sound of Alfred's fiddle.

Tears of happiness streamed from her eyes
when she saw her beloved doggie.

Then she marvelled at the beautiful duckling
and his magical fiddle-playing.

"Please don't stop," she said.
"Don't ever stop playing your wonderful music.
You are a very special duckling."

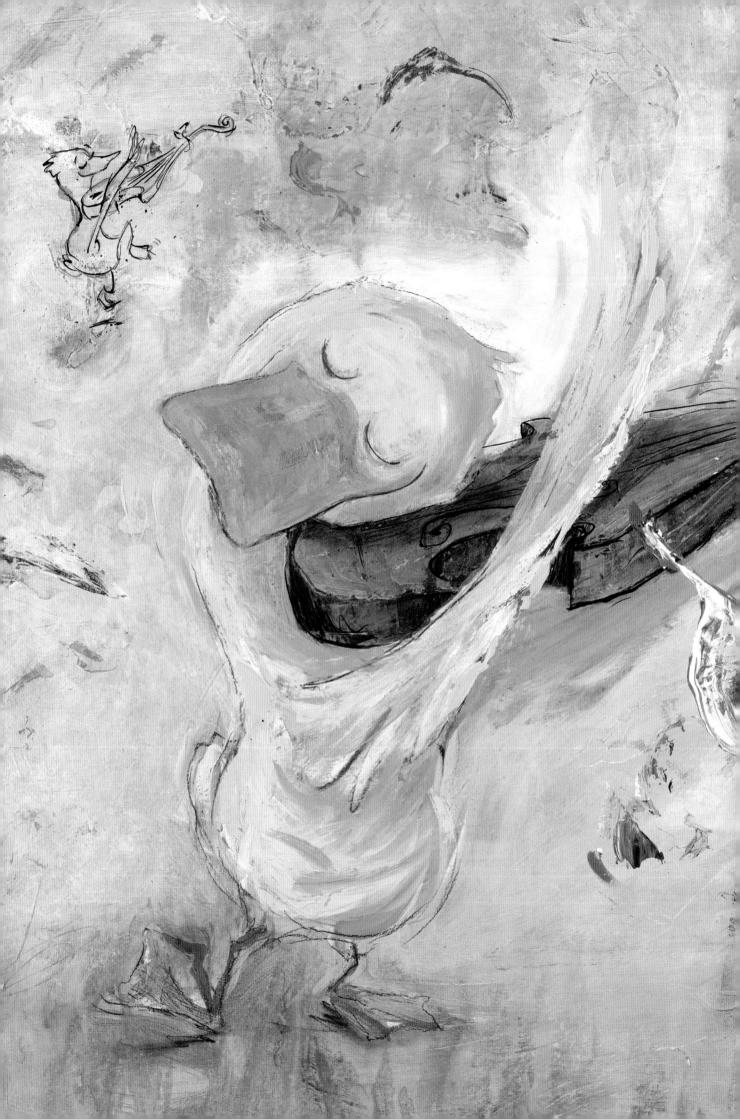

Alfred felt more joy at these strangely familiar words
than he had ever felt in his body before.
It's no surprise that the most joyous sounds of all
bounced from his fiddle!

But, you see, those sounds were a surprise, a very
unexpected surprise, to someone else…

And you can guess what will happen if
Alfred Fiddleduckling just keeps on playing!

The End